First U.S. edition 1994
Published in Great Britain in 1994 by
Walker Books Ltd., London.

Library of Congress Cataloging-in-Publication Data

Lacome, Julie.
I'm a jolly farmer / Julie Lacome.—
1st U.S. ed.
Summary: Rhyming text and illustrations follow a little girl who,
with the help of her patient dog, pretends to be a farmer, a princess,
a deep-sea diver, and little Red Riding Hood.
ISBN 1-56402-318-4
[1. Play—Fiction.   2. Imagination—Fiction.   3. Stories in rhyme.]   I. Title.
PZ8.3.L115Iam   1994
[E]—dc20   92-47374

10 9 8 7 6 5 4 3 2 1

Printed in Italy

The pictures in this book were done in paper collage.

Candlewick Press
2067 Massachusetts Avenue
Cambridge, Massachusetts 02140

I'm a Jolly Farmer

Julie Lacome

CANDLEWICK PRESS

CAMBRIDGE, MASSACHUSETTS

I'm a jolly
farmer.
Here's my
horse and cart.

Giddyup,
horsey!
It's time to
make a start.

I'm a smiling princess.
An elephant I ride.

My throne is
perched
on top of him—
I'm glad his
back's so wide!

I'm a wildlife
ranger.
I've tracked
this lion here.

He looks as though
he's fast asleep,
but I won't
get too near!

I'm a deep-sea diver.
I've met a dolphin friend.

We swim an
underwater race—
she beats me
in the end.

I'm Little Red
Riding Hood.
My granny's
sick in bed.

"What big teeth you have!" I say. I wish I hadn't come today . . .

I wish I'd stayed
at home to play...

with Fred!